Another Sommer-Time Story™

# Light Your Candle

By Carl Sommer

Illustrated by Kennon James

Advance PUBLISHING, INC. • HOUSTON

Permissions
Advance Publishing, Inc.
6950 Fulton St.
Houston, TX 77022

www.advancepublishing.com

First Edition
Printed in Singapore

**Library of Congress Cataloging-in-Publication Data**

Sommer, Carl, 1930-
  Light Your Candle / by Carl Sommer; illustrated by Kennon James. -- 1st ed.
    p. cm. -- (Another Sommer-Time Story)
    Summary: Stephanie decides to do something to get rid of crime and violence on her street, leading to a transformation of her school and neighborhood.
    ISBN 1-57537-019-0 (hardcover: alk. paper). -- ISBN 1-57537-068-9 library binding: alk. paper)
    [1. Inner cities Fiction. 2. City and town life Fiction.] I. James, Kennon, ill. II. Title. III. Series: Sommer, Carl, 1930- Another Sommer-Time Story.
PZ7.S696235Lh 2000                                                          99-36452
[E]--dc21                                                                        CIP

Another Sommer-Time Story™

# Light Your Candle

Stephanie lived in a big city with her dad, her mom, and her brother Billy.

In her neighborhood, Stephanie saw trash in the street, broken windows, houses needing

repairs, boys and girls stealing, men selling drugs, gangs fighting, and other bad things.

In Stephanie's school the students roamed around the halls, and the boys and girls fought. In the cafeteria the children threw food, and in

class the kids threw paper airplanes. Teachers were constantly yelling at the students to behave. School was not a good place to learn.

One day while Stephanie was walking with her friends Lori and Cindy, they saw a boy grab a purse from a lady and run.

Stephanie shouted, "Help! That boy just stole that woman's purse!"

Lori screamed, "Catch that thief!"

But no one tried to stop the thief. The boy ran around the corner and disappeared.

Stephanie and Lori went to the lady and asked, "Are you all right?"

"Yes dear," said the lady. "Thank you so much for trying to help."

Cindy said to her friends, "What can we do about these troublemakers?"

"I don't know," replied Stephanie, "but we should try to do something!"

"What can three girls do?" asked Lori. "It's hopeless in this big city!"

Just then a gang called the Skulls came strutting down the street with bats and sticks. They were going to have a fight with the Scorpions.

"What are you going to do about these gangs, Stephanie?" asked Lori. "Do you think you could stop them?"

Stephanie never said a word. Then Lori
added, "Even if we do something good, one little
candle in a big dark room doesn't do any good."

"I guess you're right," mumbled Stephanie.
"It's a shame we can't do something that makes a
difference."

That night as Stephanie lay in bed and
thought about the things that she had seen that
day, she wondered, "Isn't there anything we can
do?"

Everything seemed so hopeless. Finally she
fell asleep.

The next day, Stephanie said to her friends, "We need to find a way to help people like that lady yesterday."

"We can't solve everyone's problems," said Lori.

Suddenly, Stephanie stopped, and with great excitement said, "Lori, remember when you said, 'One little candle in a big dark room doesn't do any good?'"

"Yes," replied Lori.

"Well," said Stephanie, "one candle does do

some good—it lights one area. If we just help one person, we're doing something that's good."

"That's not doing much," sighed Cindy.

"It helps that one person," said Stephanie. "Besides, our doing good may encourage others to do the same. Then our one little candle will become many candles."

"You're dreaming," said Lori.

"Let's meet at my house this afternoon," said Stephanie.

"Okay," said Lori and Cindy.

When Stephanie met her friends, she said, "Let's do as much good as we can for one week."

"That's too much work," complained Lori.

"It's just for one week," said Stephanie.

"Okay," grumbled Lori. "But just *one* week!"

"Just one week for me, too!" insisted Cindy.

"Good!" said Stephanie. "What can we do?"

"Mrs. Williams just had an accident and can barely walk," said Lori. "Let's see if she needs groceries."

"That's a great idea," said Stephanie.

When Mrs. Williams opened the door, they greeted each other. Then Cindy said, "We came to help you. Do you need anything from the store?"

"Well I declare," said Mrs. Williams as she gave each of them a hug. "That's so nice of you to think of an old crippled lady like me. I do need some eggs, milk, and bread."

"We'll get the food for you," said Lori.

"Thank you," said Mrs. Williams as she shuffled to the table to get her purse. Then she gave the girls the money to buy the food.

While walking to the store, Stephanie said, "When we're finished shopping, let's clean up the trash in front of the houses. We'll call it, 'Light Your Candle Crusade.'"

"That's too much work," complained Lori.

"It sure is," added Cindy.

"We'll start with one house," said Stephanie.

"Okay," mumbled Lori and Cindy.

As they began sweeping the sidewalk, some
boys laughed at them and said, "Look at those
silly girls. I guess we got new street cleaners."

"I'm embarrassed," said Lori. "I'm quitting!"

"Me too!" said Cindy.

"You can't leave!" insisted Stephanie. "You've
made a promise to do it for one week."

"Okayyyyy," grumbled Lori and Cindy.

After cleaning the sidewalk, the girls went to clean the empty lot across the street.

"How can we get that old refrigerator on the sidewalk so the trash collectors can take it away?" asked Stephanie. "It's too heavy for us."

"Those men across the street can help us," suggested Cindy. "Why don't we ask them?"

The three girls asked the men, "Could you please help us move the refrigerator? We're trying to clean up the neighborhood."

The men smiled and said, "Sure, we'll be glad to help you move the refrigerator."

"Thank you!" said the girls.

"I think cleaning up the neighborhood is an excellent idea," said one of the men.

As the men were taking the refrigerator to the sidewalk, one of them asked, "Is there anything else we can do to help?"

"Could you please put those old tires and bed

also on the sidewalk?" asked Stephanie.

"Sure!" he replied.

"Thank you!" said Stephanie. "We're so glad you joined our Light Your Candle Crusade."

On the way home, a drug dealer said to the girls, "I've got something free for you."

"What is it?" asked Cindy.

"It will make you feel good," he said.

"We don't want your drugs," said Stephanie. "You're ruining our neighborhood."

The drug dealer got mad and yelled, "Get out

of here!  If I ever see you again, you'll be sorry!"

Stephanie and her friends ran around the corner to where they lived.  "That drug dealer is selling drugs to the kids around here," said Stephanie, "and he's threatening us."

"Let's tell our parents," said Cindy.

"That's a good idea," said Stephanie and Lori.

When Stephanie came home, her brother Billy said, "Stop making a fool of yourself by being street cleaners. Everyone's laughing at you!"

"Let them laugh," said Stephanie. "Cindy, Lori, and myself have started a Light Your Candle Crusade. We're trying to help our—"

Billy interrupted and laughed saying, "What a stupid idea."

When Stephanie's dad and mom came home, she told them what the drug dealer had said.

"What?" said her dad. "We'll put a stop to that right away! I'll get some of our friends right now! We're going to meet that drug dealer!"

"I agree," said Stephanie's mom. "We need to do something to protect our children."

"Oh good!" said Stephanie. "I'll tell Cindy and Lori so that they can tell their parents."

When Cindy and Lori's parents had heard
what happened, they became angry and met in
front of Stephanie's house. Other parents heard
about it and joined the group.

"I'm sick and tired of these drug dealers
destroying our children!" said Stephanie's dad.
"Let's do something about it!"

"I agree!" said Lori's mom. "Let's go!"

The whole group went straight to the drug

dealer. When the drug dealer saw the girls with angry parents and men coming towards him, he was scared.

Stephanie's dad put his finger in the drug dealer's face and said, "Listen, we don't ever want to see you in our neighborhood again!"

"Get out of here fast," said Lori's mom, "or we're calling the police!"

The drug dealer took off running.

The parents thanked the men who had come to help them chase the drug dealer away. Then Lori's mom said, "I'm glad we were able to do some good in our neighborhood."

Lori jumped up and yelled, "It's working!"

"It sure is!" said Stephanie. "We're beginning to light candles."

The next day at the school a fight broke out
between two boys. When a teacher tried to stop
them, one of the boys shoved the teacher aside
and kept fighting.

As the girls walked home, Stephanie asked, "What can we do to stop the fighting in school? This constant fighting makes it hard for teachers to teach."

"It sure does," said Cindy. "My dad said that our school was once the best in the city; now it's the worst!"

"I've got an idea!" said Lori. "Tomorrow is Open School Night. Let's tell our parents what's happening in our school and ask them to speak to the principal."

"Let's do it," said Cindy.

The girls went home and told their parents about the problems in their school. Stephanie and Cindy's parents were willing to go to school, but Lori's mom said, "I'm too busy. I can't go."

"Please Mom!" begged Lori. "Come just this one time."

"Okay," sighed Lori's mom.

The next night their parents spoke to the principal about the girls and the problems in their school. The principal was glad to see the parents.

"Let's have a parents' meeting," suggested Cindy's mom.

"Excellent!" said the principal. "I'll tell the PTA president about the girls and the meeting."

Many parents came to the meeting. The principal said to the parents, "This meeting was called because three of our students have started a Light Your Candle Crusade."

Then he told how the girls had cleaned up their neighborhood, went shopping for elderly neighbors, and helped rid the neighborhood of drug dealers. At the end of his speech he said, "Will Stephanie, Lori, and Cindy please come up to the platform?"

The parents stood and cheered as the three girls walked down the aisle.

After the principal thanked the girls, the president of the PTA stood up and said, "Let's make our school the best in the city. Shall we all join the Light Your Candle Crusade?"

"Yes!" shouted all the parents.

"In order for our children to learn," the president continued, "we *must* make sure we have an orderly school. Let's make some rules that will help our school to become great again. Do you have any suggestions?"

Parents stood up and said:

> Students must not fight in school.
> Students cannot run in the halls.
> Students must stay in their rooms
>     during class.
> Students must respect and obey
>     teachers.
> A parent must come to school if any
>     student disobeys the rules.

"Does everyone agree?" asked the president.
"Yes!" exclaimed all the parents.

That night the parents went home and warned their children, "You had better behave in school! We don't want to come to school because you're not obeying the rules!"

The next day the PTA president told the students the rules and warned them, "If anyone disobeys these rules, he or she will *immediately* be brought to the principal's office, and your parents will *have* to come to school!"

There was a remarkable transformation in school that day. Everyone followed the rules, except for one boy. Larry, who usually got into trouble, started a fight with another boy in the cafeteria.

Immediately the principal came and took Larry to his office. Larry had to wait in the principal's office until one of his parents came.

When Larry's mother came and found out what he had done, she apologized to the principal. Then she said, "He's going to get punished at home too. If Larry ever acts up again, make sure you let me know."

Then she took Larry home.

In school the students began to behave. Now teachers could teach and students could learn. News of what happened spread to other schools. They also began Light Your Candle Crusades.

Meanwhile, the girls continued helping people on their block. When the girls began painting the handrails for an elderly lady who could not afford a painter, the neighbors felt ashamed. Some of

the neighbors helped the girls. Others went to their landlord to ask if their houses could be fixed and painted. Their street was becoming the best-looking street in the entire neighborhood.

When a newspaper reporter heard what the girls were doing, he went to interview them. He asked, "How would someone start a Light Your Candle Crusade?"

Stephanie smiled and said, "It's easy. Find someone who is needy and go and help that one. Then try to get others to do the same. And never get discouraged."

"That's some of the best advice I've ever heard," said the reporter.

He took pictures of the girls and wrote a story about them for the Sunday newspaper. The headline read, "Three Young Girls Transform Neighborhood and School."

Now everyone in the city heard what the girls were doing. Light Your Candle Crusades were starting everywhere. The whole city was being transformed.

Now when houses needed repairs, people would fix them. When people saw someone stealing, they would yell, "Stop stealing!" When they saw anyone selling drugs or gangs fighting, they would call the police. Now people felt safe to walk in their neighborhood.

When students misbehaved, teachers would call parents. Schools were orderly and students were learning. Now children were no longer afraid to go to school.

All these things happened because one young girl decided to light her candle.

# About the Author

Carl Sommer is a devoted educator who has a passion for communicating values and practical learning skills to students.  He is dedicated to enabling young people to be successful in their personal lives and in their work.

Sommer has taught high school students in New York City, and counseled students and parents as an assistant dean of boys.  Shortly after becoming a teacher he discovered something seriously wrong with the education his students received.  Sommer began to investigate the educational system, and has personally interviewed parents, students, teachers, assistant principals, and principals.  His research also led him to work as a substitute teacher at every grade level in twenty-seven different schools in each of the five boroughs of New York City.

Identifying the problems and needs of America's students, he proceeded to craft solutions.  His exhaustive ten-year study led to his first highly-acclaimed book—*Schools in Crisis: Training for Success or Failure?*, credited with influencing school reform in many states.  (This book is now free at www.advancepublishing.com.)

Sommer has witnessed some of the tragic events that are described in *Light Your Candle*.  His hope is that this book will inspire individuals and communities to provide a safe environment for its children, and an educational system that properly prepares them for their future.